Cornelius Francis Thomas

**Genealogy of the Boarman Family**

Cornelius Francis Thomas

**Genealogy of the Boarman Family**

ISBN/EAN: 9783741186790

Manufactured in Europe, USA, Canada, Australia, Japa

Cover: Foto ©Andreas Hilbeck / pixelio.de

Manufactured and distributed by brebook publishing software
(www.brebook.com)

Cornelius Francis Thomas

**Genealogy of the Boarman Family**

# GENEALOGY

OF THE

# BOARMAN FAMILY.

––––––––

BALTIMORE:
JOHN MURPHY & CO.
1897.

TO THE MEMBERS

OF THE

# BOARMAN FAMILY,

ANCIENT, HONORABLE, TRUE;

ESPECIALLY FROM AMONG THEM TO HER WHO GAVE ME BIRTH:

ARE THESE PAGES AFFECTIONATELY DEDICATED.


C. F. THOMAS,

Baltimore, May 12, 1897.                    *Rector of the Cathedral.*

# THE BOARMAN FAMILY.

The Boarmans are of English origin. Their home was in Devonshire and Somersetshire Counties of England. It is related that the inhabitants of these counties were annoyed by boars, and that, for their services in exterminating these animals, and in ridding the natives of their ravages, the family acquired the name of Boarman and the right to a heraldic shield and crest. This coat of arms and crest is thus described: "The crest is a bull's head: below it is a shield with a broad bar passing through it from top to bottom diagonally: on the bar are three boars' heads: above and below this bar are arrow heads: and around the shield is certain colored work indicating the heraldic standing of the family."

In the early records of Maryland Colonial times the name is written in several ways, owing doubtless to the habit of phonetic spelling or, perhaps, to the ignorance of the clerks. So we find Boreman, Boarman, Boareman, once or twice Bowman, then Bosman, the *s* being the present printing for the manuscript *z* or *r*. But the proper way is Boarman.

The first of the family who came to the Province of Maryland was William Boarman, and that was in 1645. For in the Proceedings of the Provincial Court there is recorded, on May 28, 1650, a deposition of "William Boreman aged 20 yeares," to the effect that, about 1645, he was aboard a "certain Pynnace then riding in St. Inigoes Creeke," and that this boat was in command of a Mr. Monroe.

In 1648 William Boreman was one of the jurors at the session of the Provincial Court held at St. Maries' in February; and his name appears at various other sessions and in other capacities of the same court. On October 24, of the year 1648, he is party in a case wherein an amicable agreement was entered into. November 19, 1649, the Court ordered 60 pounds of tobacco to be paid to him for three days' attendance at a trial as witness for the plaintiff. And on February 25, 1649, he gives valuable testimony for the defendant as to the writing, signing and delivery of a certain deed.

The deposition above referred to tells us that, while the vessel on which he had been in 1645 was in St. Inigoes Creek, under the command of Monroe, "Mr. Richard Ingle rode in the said creek and the said Monroe seemed to make very little resistance to him, & was then employed in the wars against this Government." Our ancestor was a prisoner on this vessel, having "been taken at Mr. Copleyes House at Portoback (Portobacco) and brought to St. Maries." Reference, of course, is here made to Clayborne's and Ingle's attempts to undermine Lord Baltimore's rights and government.

March 11, 1651, William Boreman appoints Mr. John Medcalfe as his attorney in all causes at court wherein the said Boreman is or shall be concerned, and on April 6, 1654, he appoints Mr. Richard Hotchkeyes to that position and office. These gentlemen do not seem to have had a sinecure, as William figures in many cases. On March 22, 1651, Michael Baysey acknowledges judgment to him for 356 pounds of tobacco, and on January 21, 1652, he and Francis Vanenden bind themselves and heirs to the sum of 2,000 pounds of tobacco as the final end and settlement of all differences between them.

The most interesting data about him are gathered from the sessions of 1655, in one of which "William Boreman confesseth in Court that he's a Roman Catholick and that he was borne and

bred so." (That was in the time of the rule of the Parliament Commissioners.) The other shows him as having aided Governor Stone in his uprising against the Lord Proprietary. For "William Boreman being convicted of Compliance with Captain William Stone in the last rebellion submitteth himself to the mercy of the Court: and thereupon (the Court) remitteth the publick offense, and amerceth him to pay 1000 pds. Tobacco towards the damage sustained by said rebellion and to remain in sheriffes custody until said Boreman shall pay said sum or give security for the payment." For William's release we doubtless feel grateful to Nathaniell Burroughs, who "engageth himself as security with said William for the payment of the sum abovesaid and for his Good abearance to the present Government in the penalty of one hundred pound Sterling."

The acts of the Council give us some insight into the prominent part he played in the events of those days when Cecilius Calvert was the Lord Proprietary and Charles Calvert was Governor (1661–1675). His name is now almost invariably written Boarman, and he is called Captain, afterwards Major.

The Council held at Spesutia, May 13, 1661, took some action to afford aid against Indian and other lawless attacks against the people and government of the Province. Fifty men were ordered by the Assembly to be sent to Sasquehannough Forte to aid the Sasquehannoughs. Captain John Odber was placed in command, and, of the fifty, four were selected from Captain William Boarman's company. In 1666 he was Captain of the government militia, and the next year was appointed to raise a company against the Indians. Again, on April 10, 1686, the Council orders Major Boarman to go and take measures to keep the English from annoying the Indians.

While engaged in these military enterprises, he also was commissioned in civil capacities, for in 1667 he was one of those who were sent to lay off and apportion the lands acquired from the

Indians by treaty of peace. These lands lay between Mattawoman Creek and Pascattaway Creek. During this year, too, he was one of the coroners for the upper part of St. Mary's County, while in 1664, May 26, together with Stephen Horsey and Captain William Thorne, Captain William Boarman, Gent<sup>m</sup>, formed the commission empowered to grant lands (for six months) to all who wanted to come to the Province from Northton County, otherwise called Accomack, in Virginia.

The colonists were engaged, when not at war, in trading with the Indians. The Captain, on March 25, 1663, was licensed also to trade with them, but he bound himself (Captain William Boarman, Gent<sup>n</sup>) "to pay to the Lord Proprietary in the just and full sum of 500 pounds Ster. Eng. money, if he does not yield up to the Lord Prop. or his heirs, the 10<sup>th</sup> part in weight & value of all commodities traded with the Indians." I find also that the Assembly, in November, 1682, gave Major Boarman permission to trade with the Indians in Calvert County, in Ann Arundell and St. Mary's Counties.

About this time he is accused, in conjunction with Darnell and Edward Pye, of inciting the Senecas to kill the Protestants. The hue and cry were raised that these were in danger, and that the Catholics aimed to get entire control of the government and were enlisting the Indians on their side. The better to secure their aid, the Catholics were alleged to have impressed the Indians with the fear that the Protestants were going to kill them. The three men just mentioned were accused of being the leaders, and Indians were brought in to swear that Mr. Boarman cursed (God Dam) and had declared to the Indians that the Protestants were going to kill the Catholics and then the Indians. But the Council, after due examination and deliberation, cleared these gentlemen of the charge, and so declared on March 28, 1689.

A commission had been apppointed and had gone to Zachiah Fort to interrogate the Indians about this matter. "The Emperor

called the great men who declared that Coll. Darnell & Coll. Pye and Major Boarman had no Conference with the Indians on the subject in question and said that the Indian, named Wawoostongh, the one who reported the words and trouble to Mr. Burr Harris, was a runaway from them and an Idle person." Notwithstanding the favorable judgment passed by the Council, I find Matthew Tennison, of St. Mary's County, in December, 1690, repeating the same accusation under oath.

Finally, the Acts of Assembly present our ancestor as taking part in its deliberations. In March, 1671, he was Deputy for St. Mary's County, in the assembly held at St. Mary's town, and was on several honorable committees and commissions. Besides this, these Acts tell us that in 1669 (April–May) Captain William Boreman received pay in tobacco for services rendered the Province. In 1676 Major William Boreman received portion of the tobacco publicly levied as taxes, and on September 9, 1681, the Upper House wrote on his petition that it thought the 2,000 pounds of tobacco voted November, 1678, and allowed Major William Boarman for his services to his country when sent against the Nanticoke Indians, was far short of his merits, as they had used him as their only interpreter from 1675 to 1681, in the negotiations had with the Choptico, the Mattawoman, the Promunckey, the Nangemy, the Mattapenny and Pascattaway Indians, and it recommends the Lower House to make up the deficiency and vote the appropriation. This was discussed at several sessions from September to November and finally passed. Moreover, Major William Boareman is recorded in other different places as having been paid now 1,400 pounds, now 800 pounds, and again 2,400 pounds of tobacco; while in October, 1682, the same person, "late high Sherif of St. Mary's Co., prays for compensation of 1000 pds. Tobacco for the execution of William Sewick, and for the custody of George Godfrey who had been recently released by act of the Council."

I now meet with the entry that, in 1682, a Mr. William Boreman, Sr., is on a commission to lay out some lands. The following episode is also recorded. It appears that a William Goodwin, aged sixteen years, had bound himself to Captain Joseph Eaton for the purpose of learning the art of navigation. The voyage was made to Maryland. But, when they got there, William Goodwin was sold as a slave to Thomas Gerard. His sister, Mrs. Audrey Beale, wife of Captain Richard Beale, who was one of His Majesty's Brigadiers, petitions the King for his release, and in the petition it is stated that this boy is the nephew of William Boreman, Sr. The Provincial Commissioners recommended that Eaton deliver the boy to his agent for transportation back to England. But the Governor prevailed on the petitioner "to let this Business fall," December, 1684. Thirdly, William Boreman, Jr., is one of the Gentlemen Justices of St. Mary's County during 1679 and 1680. From this I judge that there was a second William Boarman in Maryland, younger and coming later than the other to the Province. This conclusion is certain, not only from the above statement, but also because the study of the grants of land made to them, and of the wills they made, reveal two of the same name existing contemporaneously and yet of no blood relationship. The first William—the earliest one on record, who died in 1709—had no son by the name of William, while the second one had. Hence, the second was called senior. Besides, the first one, in a codicil to his will, leaves a testimony of his esteem and friendship to William Boarman, "his true friend." Therefore, in what follows I shall designate the first as Number 1 and the other as Number 2.

## LAND GRANTS.

I have before me copies of various patents and grants of land which I secured from the Land Office at Annapolis, as well as copies of some and extracts from others of the wills made by the

family up to the year 1800. From them I have studied out their various possessions and have been enabled to form a pretty correct line of descent for the present survivors. Some names are not mentioned, and the marriages with other families are not studied all through, partly for lack of access to a few of the descendants, but chiefly because the church records were destroyed in a fire many years ago at St. Thomas' Manor, and the court records were lost in a similar way by the destruction of the Charles County Court House at Port Tobacco some few years since.

I have two series of land grants, and I am confident they are exact. William Boarman, No. 1, sometimes called Major, at other times Captain, obtained the first grant of land, and that was in 1661. At this time—February 17—he obtained a patent for "Boarman's Rest," of 1,000 acres, adjoining the land of William Calvert, and on June 19, 1661, for 50 acres, called "Assention," adjoining the land of Thomas Gerrard. He, however, surrendered up said grants into the Secretary's office, when a new survey was made and a new grant issued to him for above named lands by the name of "Boarman's Rest," 767 acres, and lying in St. Mary's County. This was March 9, 1672, the resurvey being made May 10, 1670. (This part of St. Mary's County was afterwards ceded to form part of Charles County.) "Boarman's Rest" lay with Zachiah Swamp as its western boundary. I have the courses and distances of this tract, as well as of the others which follow; but the names of the creeks and runs have changed, and I am unable to locate them very definitely.

In 1699, October 3, another tract was surveyed for him of 857 acres, called "Addition," adjoining "Boarman's Manor," being in St. Mary's County, now called Charles County, on the southeast side of Zachiah Swamp, in the woods. It was around about "Indian Fields" and "Daly's Rest" and "Boarman's Reserve," and near Mr. John Bowling's land called "Charley."

The same year there was granted the Major a patent for 1,000 acres, called "His Lordship's Favor," lying on Zachiah Manor. But this was assigned, on September 2, 1699, to Hugh Tears, of Charles County, and, having been by him bequeathed to his wife Eleanor and Elizabeth, his daughter, the patent was issued to these two on July 10, 1705.

Again, 780 acres, on the east side of Zachiah Swamp, and bounded by Mr. William Williams' land called "Lanternam" (which afterwards became the Major's), and lying in St. Mary's County, were granted Major William Boarman July 5, 1686, and called "Wardle." They had been surveyed August 29, 1673.

The last patent I notice was issued October 10, 1686 (being surveyed November 2, 1685), for 588 acres, called "Boarman's Reserve," and bounded by Richard Edelin's White Oak, by a tree of a parcel of land called "Lanternam," and by another standing by Zachiah Swamp side.

Now this is the tract obtained by William Boarman, Sr., or No. 2, viz.:

"Boarman's Content," consisting of 1,000 acres, which had been granted July 24, 1661, to George Thomson (a gift from the Lord Proprietary, as one of his faithful followers), and known as "Thomson's Rest." Thomson sold the same to William Fox, of Bristol, England, merchant. But Fox failed to pay the rent for the said "Thomson's Rest" (so the records state). Then William Boarman, paying to the Receiver General of the Province 20,000 pounds of tobacco, which the first William Boarman was not able to do, a grant was issued to him for that tract resurveyed and called "Boarman's Content." It was situated in Charles County, on the east side of Piscataway River, on the north side of Piscataway Creek, and adjoining "Luke Barbour's Land." It was resurveyed December 21, 1671, and patent issued on March 1, 1673.

William Boarman, Jr., received, November 10, 1703, a patent for "Timberwell," 200 acres, which had been surveyed for him on June 2. It was in Charles County, on the east side of Zachiah Swamp, and, from the description, contiguous to land held by the other Boarman.

The same William, Jr., and his wife Monica were granted a piece of land in St. Mary's County, next to a tract held by Ozwald Neal and called "Saint Winefred's Freehold," and comprising 263 acres, which was called "Saint Dorothy." The survey was made June 25, 1714, and patent issued April 10, 1715.

Lastly, on June 10, 1734, William Boarman obtained a patent for land resurveyed April 14, 1725. According to the records, a patent was issued to his grandfather May 10, 1676, for 3,333 acres, called "Boarman's Manor," which was resurveyed by his son, William Boarman, and still called "Boarman's Manor," November 10, 1719; but he died before the patent was issued, and now his son William applied for the same. The resurvey was made, and Boarman's Manor included 3,978 acres, A. D. 1734.

All told, I think about thirty tracts of land were in the possession of the Boarmans. Some were new surveys of old grants and others were new accessions. The wills I have seen make mention of "Boarman's Enlargement," "Boarman's Meadows," "Boarman's Help," "George's Rest," "Calvert's Hope," but I do not know when or how acquired. But I am quite sure none of these lands are in the hands of any members of the family with whom I am acquainted. The lands they acquired at first were situated in that part of the country which was ceded to the Province by treaty with the Indians after these had been brought to submission by the Government. The lands of William No. 1, lay in the present eastern part of Charles County, and those of William No. 2, to the west. Boarman's Manor was in the centre, westward.

Interesting as all this is, more interesting, because more personal, is the tracing of the lines of descent. This is easy up to 1773. The wills afford abundant data. But after the Revolution the family began to scatter. Even then it is not very hard to trace the several main branches, though some individuals have strayed beyond reach. If ever they see these pages, they may themselves be able to trace their connection with the parent stems. The following is the first attempt I know of to write the Boarman genealogy. Will any one make it more perfect?

# GENEALOGY.

**WILLIAM BOARMAN, No.** 1, departed this life in 1709, and, by will, left 1,000 pounds of tobacco to the Church and a similar amount to the poor. He made provision that his son Benedict and his heirs should keep in repair the chapel that "is now standing on my dwelling plantation," and, in case of any neglect on the part of this son or his heirs, then the plantation called "Boarman's Rest" shall fall to the next surviving heir. To his son Francis Ignatius he gave "Lanternam," and to his son John Baptist part of "George's Rest." The chapel just mentioned is supposed to have stood on or near the site of the present church of Bryantown, Charles County, Md.

His wife was Mary Boarman; his sons were Benedict, Francis Ignatius and John Baptist; his daughters were Clare, Mary and Ann Brooke.

**Benedict's** line is as follows, with Benedict Leonard as his son. I have found no other offspring mentioned.

Benedict Leonard died in 1757, and devised "Boarman's Rest," "Boarman's Enlargement" and "Boarman's Addition."

Issue—Sons: Benedict,     Daughters: Catharine Gardiner,
             Leonard,                 Mary Boarman,
             Basil,                  Elener Boarman,
             Richard,                 Jane Boarman.
             George,
             Joseph.

*A.* Leonard, son of Benedict Leonard, died 1794. His wife was named Elizabeth (*née* Jenkins); his sons were Joseph, Charles, Sylvester; his daughters, Catharine Gardiner, Monica Edelin and Anne Gardiner. Joseph was appointed sole executor.

(1). Joseph (son of Leonard), whose will was made November 14, 1825, begot:

   (*a*). Benedict L.,     Sarah E. Posey,
   (*b*). Joseph S.,     Catharine M. Boarman.
   Frederick M., (grandson, Joseph A. Knott),
   Walter F., (granddaughter, Sarah J. Posey).

      (*a*). The wife of Benedict L. (Rebecca) died January 29, 1857.

      (*b*). Joseph S., who married a Miss Fairfax, of Virginia, and who died in 1854, left issue:

         Walter Fairfax,     Sarah,
         Frederick,     Maria,
         Joseph S.

            Walter Fairfax (M. D.) begot:
              John Walter,     Mary Julia,
              Joseph S.,     Ellen Rose,
              William Ignatius, Emily.
              Albert.

            William Ignatius is now living and has a family at Bryantown, Md. He is a physician.

(2). Charles (son of Leonard) married a Miss Edelin and died in 1819. He taught at Georgetown College from 1797–1819, and is buried in the College grave-yard. His issue was:

      (*a*). Charles, Admiral, U. S. Navy, who married a Miss Anna Abell, of St. Mary's County, and died at Martinsburg, W. Va., not long ago. Their daughter, Miss Anna Boarman, lives in Martinsburg.

      (*b*). Dr. Joseph George, who, in 1812, married Miss Lucy Dyer. His issue:

Sylvester Baker (died November 10, 1890),

| | | |
|---|---|---|
| Thomas D., | | Rose, |
| William D., | Dead. | Susannah, |
| Robert, | | Mary, |

Dead. (for Thomas D., William D., Robert)

Dead. (for Susannah, Mary)

Sylvester Baker married Maria L. Morgan.

Children : William W.,
Charles V. (M. D.),
George C.,
All living in Washington, D. C.

(c). Courtney Boarman, who married Mary Ede-lin, with offspring Leonard and Thomas.

(d). Aloysius Boarman, who married Miss Gar-diner.

(e). Anna Boarman, who married Samuel Queen.

Children : Joseph,      Maria,
Thomas.      Sarah,
Jane.

(f). Elizabeth Boarman, who married Marsham Queen.

Children : Charles (M. D.),      Marcellina,
Theodore.      Rose.

(g). Sallie Boarman (single).

(3). Rev. Sylvester Boarman (son of Leonard), who studied at Liège, Belgium, became a priest ; came to Maryland as a priest in 1774 ; exercised the ministry in Harford County, Md., from 1793–1797, when he was transferred to Charles County, and died at Newtown in 1811.

B. Richard, son of Benedict Leonard, went to St. Mary's County, and died there in 1782 ; he left a widow, Ann Boarman, and three daughters, Catharine, Louisa and Ann, making in his will some bequests to his sisters, Elinor and Jane, and to his nephew, Benedict, son of his deceased brother George.

*C.* George Boarman, son of Benedict Leonard, died in 1768.
His wife was Mary; his brother was Richard; his sons
were Benedict and Aloysius, and his daughters were
Elizabeth, Eleanor and Mary.

(*a*). Benedict died in 1815.

| Issue: Richard Benedict, | Elizabeth, |
|---|---|
| George S. | Catharine, |
| | Mary. |

(*b*). Elizabeth died (unmarried) in 1825.

**Francis Ignatius,** second son of William, No. 1, had but one son,
as far as ascertainable, and that was *Ignatius,* who died in
1743, mentioning in his will four sons, Gerard, William,
Francis and John.

I. John, who died in 1750, left a widow, Elizabeth; sons, Richard, Joseph, Raphael and Bennet; daughter, Henrietta
Tomson.

A. Raphael died in 1781. Wife, Elinor; sons, Joseph and
John Baptist; daughters, Elizabeth, Rebecca,
Juliana, Sarah. (The sons were not yet eighteen
years old.)

(1). John B. died in Georgetown, D. C., in 1813,
and in his will made bequests to his cousin,
Raphael W. Boarman, of Georgetown, and
to his nephew, Raphael Horace Boarman,
of Charles County. The lands devised were
"Addition" and "Bachelor's Hope," the last
having been purchased from John Leiper.

(2). Elizabeth married Mr. Underwood (Charles
County).

(3) Rebecca married Mr. Edelin.

(4). Sarah married Mr. Barrett. (The last two lived
in Georgetown.)

*B.* Bennet's issue was Raphael and John H.

 (1). Raphael (of Bennet) died in 1807.

Son: Raphael Hoskins.
Daughters: Mary Ann Fenwick,<br>Eleanor Phebe Fenwick,<br>Dorothy Smith Boarman,<br>Ann Wharton Boarman,<br>Elizabeth Harriet Boarman.<br>The wife of Raphael Hoskins was E. M.<br>Boarman. Elizabeth Harriet was a<br>nun at Georgetown, D. C., and her<br>name in religion was Sister Bene-<br>dicta.

 (2). John H. Boarman (brother of Raphael and nephew of Joseph) died in 1804. His wife was named Sarah Teresa; his sons were George W., Bennet H., John Baptist and Michael; his daughters were Mildred, Matilda, Mary Louisa and Juliana. Lands devised were "Calvert's Hope," "Boarman's Rest," "Boarman's Meadows," "Boarman's Help" and "Boarman's Enlargement."

II. Francis (son of Ignatius) went to St. Mary's County, and died there in 1773. It seems his wife had died before him, for he leaves his orphan children to the care of others, viz.:

His son Francis Ignatius was intrusted to Mr. George Slye.

His son John was intrusted to Mr. Richard Boarman.

His daughter Sarah was intrusted to Mrs. Henrietta Plowden.

**John Baptist,** third son of William, No. 1. His sons, as I glean from the will of Richard Bennet Boarman (son of John Baptist), were Richard Bennet, Joseph and Raphael.

Richard Bennet. His wife, Mary Ann; sons, Raphael and
Richard Bennet; daughters, Ellender and Elizabeth.
He made his will in 1752 and died in 1758.

(a). Raphael probably married Elizabeth Thompson. Died
in 1806.

Their issue: Raphael, Jr., Ensign, U. S. A., in 1776.

(b). Richard Bennet, First Lieutenant in 1776.

This line I have been unable to trace further.

## THE BALTIMORE BRANCH.

In 1805, April 15, Ignatius Boarman was married in Baltimore to
Mary Kintz. He had been some little time a resident of this city.
He was born at Port Tobacco, Charles County, Md.; but his father
died when he was quite a boy, and Ignatius was about sixteen years of
age when he came to Baltimore. His mother married again in Washington a man named Harding. I feel confident he was the son of
William who was the son of the Ignatius who died in 1743. I am sure
he descended from one of the lines above described, because his eldest
child and daughter, Rebecca, my maternal grandmother, used to tell
me that, though she married a George Boarman, of Charles County,
he was not related to her. Now this George, as will be seen below,
was a lineal descendant of William Boarman, whom I have above
designated as No. 2.

Ignatius, with all his children save Rebecca and another, migrated
to the West sometime between about 1838 or 1840. His
issue and their whereabouts follow:

(a). Rebecca, born February 8, 1806, and died in October, 1887,
married George Boarman, of Charles County, in
1821.

Issue: (1). Celestia, born 1823 (now living), who married a Mr. Swift, of Massachusetts.

(2). John, born 1825.

(3). Henry Augustine, born 1827.

(4). Mary Clare, born 1839, who in 1856 married Cornelius Thomas, and died in October, 1874.

Issue (now living): Rev. C. F. Thomas,
Norbourn Thomas
(married),
Claude Thomas,
Charles Thomas.

(*b*). William, born 1808, whose wife's Christian name was Agnes.
Issue: William Alfred, now living in Washington, D. C.,
and a daughter who entered a Religious Sisterhood; Charles Francis, born 1839 (?).

(*c*). Ignatius, Jr., born 1809, who married (1831) Sarah Ann Warner.
Issue: John Warner,        Margaret Louise,
Joseph Aloysius.     Mary Elizabeth.

(*d*). Charles Sylvester (M. D.), born 1816, living now in Boonville, Mo.
Issue: By marriage with Eliza Adelaide Smith, of Virginia, in 1840—Mary Ellen, Emily, Charles, Robert, Mary Lee, Anna, Rev. Marshall Boarman, S. J., Frank and Jerome.
By marriage with Pauline Sloan, in St. Louis, 1861—Anthony, Thomas, James, Adelaide, Elizabeth, George, Florence, Willis and Augusta.

(*e*). John Athanasius, born 1818, who married Jane Dunklin.

(*f*). Jerome George, born 1820, who married (1856) Laura A. Horner, of Kansas City, Mo., and is still living.
Issue: Jerome Augustine,        Mary Ada,
John Thomas.         Julia Henrietta.

(*g*). Cecilia Agnes, born 1822 (dead).

(*h*). Thomas M., born 1824, who married Mary Mills (1854); lived in San Francisco.

Issue: (1). Louise, who married James B. Metcalfe.
Children: Thomas Orent,
James Vernon.
(2). Marguerite.
(3). Thomas Mills, who married Sarah Buckley,
with issue as follows:
Thomas Mills,      Mabelle,
Marguerite,      Beatrice.

(i). Frances Helen.
There is also in Cathedral records the baptism of Margaret Cecilia, born 1852 of Jeremiah and Margaret Boarman. Who they are and where they are, I don't know.

John, a brother of Ignatius, Sr.

Mary, a sister of Ignatius, Sr. She married a Mr. Coombs, of Kentucky.

Elizabeth, sister also of Ignatius, Sr., who married a Mr. Reynolds, of Bardstown, and whose son was Bishop Reynolds, of Charleston, S. C.


## THE HARFORD COUNTY BRANCH.

Robert Boarman married Mary Wheeler in 1790. Who his father was and where he was born is not apparent. He was a trustee of the Catholic Church at Hickory, Md., from 1819 to 1821.
His children were: William,
Benjamin Wheeler,
Edward,
Robert,
Sarah (who married Mr. Robinson),
Louisa (who married Mr. Scott),
Catharine (who married Dr. Bussey),
Mary Ann (who married Mr. Moore).

(*a*). Benjamin W., born 1800, married Jane Caroline Jameson, of Charles County, and died in 1869.

Issue: E. Alexander, born 1837, died 1876.

Robert R. Boarman, a distinguished attorney-at-law, of Towson, Md.

Columbus, who lives in the State of Texas.

Frank (now dead).

(*b*). Edward married a Miss Martha C. Morgan and then a Miss McAttee.

I find the record of one child, James Lee, son of Edward and Martha C. Morgan, born in January, 1849.

(*c*). Catharine was married in 1837 to Dr. Henry G. Bussey.

In the grave-yard of St. Ignatius' Church, Hickory, a stone bears the inscription: "Caroline, wife of A. J. Boarman, died 1806."

St. Vincent's Church records mention the baptism, January 3, 1843, of Eliza A. Boarman, wife of Dr. Boarman. (She was the first wife of Dr. Charles Boarman, now of Boonville, Mo.)

---

THE DESCENDANTS OF WILLIAM BOARMAN, SR., OR NO. 2.

**WILLIAM BOARMAN**, Sr., or No. 2. This William died in 1720, and his Will mentions his wife, Mary, and sons, William, Thomas James and Joseph; daughters, Sarah, Jane and Mary.

**William**, Jr., who died in 1729; wife, Monica. They had three children, William, James, Elizabeth. He mentions an uncle, Benjamin, and a cousin, Raphael Neal.

**William**, grandson of William, Sr., died in 1767. He it was who had renewed his grandfather's patent for "Boarman's Manor." His wife was named Winnifred; children, William, Edward and Mary Ann.

William, great-grandson of William, Sr., whose wife was
Dorothy, died in 1780.

Issue: Ignatius,     Mary Ann,
   William,     Sussannah.
   Clement,
   Girard.

 Girard S. (son of Girard), who died in 1840.  Wife,
   Catharine.
   Son: George, who married Rebecca Boarman
    in Baltimore in 1821.  (My grandfather
    and grandmother.)  Issue (pp. 20, 21).
  Daughter: Elizabeth Loretto, who married a Mr.
    McWilliams.  Their son lives now in
    Baltimore with his wife and children.

**Joseph** (son of William, Sr.), must have died unmarried.  Dying
in 1730, he left all he had to his mother, Mary, and to his
brother, Thomas James.

**Thomas James** (son of William, Sr.), died in 1785.  Wife's name,
Jean; sons, Thomas James, Joseph, Edward, Raphael, James
and Rev. John C.; daughter, Sarah.

(1). Rev. John C. Boarman, born 1743, studied at Liège; returned
to Maryland a priest in 1774, and was buried at
Newtown, Md., in 1794.

(2). Raphael, born 1749, died 1829.
Raphael's wife, Mary, 1765–1786.
Raphael's son, Walter.

(3). Joseph died in 1797, and left three sons and three daughters.

(a). Henry, First Lieutenant, Third Maryland Battalion.

(b). Michael, who died in 1832 and left all he had to his
wife, Teresa.

(c). John Chrysostom, who died in 1844 and left one
son, Joseph, and a daughter, Adeline.

Edward begot Mary, who married Raphael Boarman (page 24, (2)).

Wilfrid, who died unmarried.

James, who married Mary Bradford (whose mother was
Boarman).

Issue—Eliza, who married Charles Lancaster.

Mary, " Lewis A. Jenkins.

Henrietta, " Dr. William Queen.

Eleanor and Harriet died unmarried.

(James was the grandfather of Mrs. Faxon and Mrs. John C. Thompson
of Baltimore).

William's issue was Ignatius, William, Clement, Girard, Mary Ann and
Susannah.

Girard married Miss Sewalk, of Virginia, with issue.

a), Girard S., whose first wife was Mary Queen.

Children—(1) George, who married Rebecca Boarman in Baltimore in 1821. (My grandfather and grand-
mother.) Issue (pp. 20, 21).

(2) Mary Ann and Susan, who both became Visitation
Nuns at Georgetown.

Second wife was Catherine Neale, by whom came Elizabeth Loretto, who
married a Mr. McWilliams. Their son lives now in Baltimore with
his wife and children.

b) Ann, who married Francis Queen.

Issue—Dr. William Queen, who married Henrietta, daughter of
James Boarman, as above. These are the grand-
parents of Sister Xavier Queen. (Park Avenue
Convent).

c) Mary, who married Mr. Wright, of Virginia, whose daughter
became a Nun at Georgetown.

There is on record the will of John Boarman, of Thomas. I am unable to place him. He died in 1813. His wife was Monica; his sons were Francis, Tobias, Aloysius (1794–1798) and George; his daughters were Catharine, Matilda, Mary Ann and Martha.

Francis married Monica Hagon, of Kentucky.    **1909784**

> Issue: (1). Teresa, who married Mr. Waltham, and lived in Missouri.
>
> (2). Another daughter married Joseph Thompson.
>
> (3). A third daughter married Thomas Bowling.
>
> > Both of Charles County.
>
> (4). George and (5) Matilda remained single.
>
> (6). Tobias, who married Sarah Ann Edelin.
>
> > Issue : Francis (never married).
> >
> > Mary H. (living in Washington, D. C.).
> >
> > Robert I., whose three sons and one daughter live in Baltimore.
> >
> > Another son married Mary E. McClelland, of Richmond, Ind. His widow lives in Washington.

### UNCLASSED.

I. In Charles County :

> (1). Eleanor, sister of Leonard, Richard and George, died unmarried, and left her estate to her nephews, Joseph, Charles (sons of Leonard) and Benedict (son of George), and to her nieces, Mary (daughter of George) and Teresa (?).
>
> (2). Eleanor, whose children were Richard Holmes and Mary Holmes B.
>
> (3). John W., whose wife, Elizabeth, daughter of Alexius Lancaster, died January 29, 1857, aged thirty years.
>
> (4). Joseph Millrons, of Thomas.
>
> (5). Alexius Boarman, who was living (and of age) in 1816.

II. In District of Columbia:

    (1). Susan Boarman (died 1822), whose mother was Elizabeth and whose sister was Mary Ann.

    (2). Raphael Horace Boarman, of Charles County, died in Georgetown in 1861. His sister was Mrs. Fenwick. He probably was a son of Raphael (of Bennet).

    (3). Richard A. Boarman (died 1869) and his wife, Elizabeth, who survived him.

    (4). Sarah Boreman, of Georgetown (died 1870), whose niece was Elizabeth Young.

    (5). Charles L. Boarman (died 1870) and his wife, Mary, who survived him.

———

Perhaps more and fuller details of family history may in time be forthcoming. What I have gathered will serve as a basis for other compilations. I do not pretend to have gathered all—only what is found in printed records.

It is interesting to know that during the Revolutionary War some members of the family were not absent from the American ranks. When filling vacancies in the military, the Committee of Observation for Charles County recommended Raphael Boarman, Jr., Ensign, and Richard Bennet Boarman, First Lieutenant, for promotion. These were accordingly appointed March 7, 1776.

The Council of Safety, June, 1776, ordered Henry Boarman, First Lieutenant, of Charles County, to be paid £46.10. He belonged to the Third Maryland Battalion of the "Flying Camp" from 1776 to ——.

Besides this, in a memorial gotten up in 1775 and presented to the Charles County authorities, Gerrard Boarman, Henry Boarman, Edward Boreman, Sr., Richard Boarman and Raphael Boarman are among the signers to the petition, and it recommended "That

Patrick Graham, of Port Tobacco, feel the mercy and clemency of the Authorities and be restored to freedom."

(1). Gerrard was the son of Ignatius, who died in 1750.

(2). Henry, First Lieutenant, son of Joseph, who died in 1797.

(3). Edward Boreman, Sr., son of William, who died in 1767. He had a son, who is mentioned as Edward Boarman, Jr.

(4). Richard Bennet, First Lieutenant, and Raphael were sons of Richard Bennet, who died in 1758.

(5). Raphael Boarman, Jr., son of the Raphael just mentioned. Thus both lines of the family were represented in the War of the Revolution.

I subjoin a copy of a letter written by Rev. Sylvester Boarman to Archbishop Carroll:

" I left Baltimore yesterday evening in great trouble of mind. Our affairs in Harford in a most deplorable state. I am without a shilling to go through all the labour and hardships of my extensive Missions and without the least assistance spiritual or temporal. Our new Trustees are chosen and have nothing done for me. Either I must have both farms restored to my sole management immediately that I may provide in future for myself or my pension 35 (pounds) for the past year must be furnished without delay as I am really suffering for necessaries. If I may be allowed to make a choice, I would rather retire from both farms with a pension as above of thirty five pounds per annum, and give up the farms to some vigorous active American, English or Irish gentleman, who can also assist me on the Missions sometimes as occasions might require; for I never will agree they should remain in or hereafter be put again into French hands. Whatever reform in your management may be decided on, I beg you will be so kind as to furnish me a Gentleman able and proper to assist me on this mission as I cannot hereafter go through the fatigues of it alone. I will be very thankful for an answer by the first occasion. I am with due esteem your very humble servant

"SYLV / BOARMAN."

In the small work *Old Catholic Maryland and Its Early Jesuit Missionaries*, the Rev. William P. Treacy, on page 152, gives a brief account of Father John Boarman's life and labors. But he states that he had two brothers in the Society (of Jesus), Charles and Sylvester. Now I believe this statement cannot be verified. Father John was the son of Thomas James Boarman (son of William, Sr., or William, No. 2), while Father Sylvester was the son of Leonard, of the line of William, No. 1. They were not even cousins. Father John Boarman had no brother by the name of Sylvester or Charles. Charles Boarman was, indeed, a brother of Sylvester, but was not a priest. He was educated with Sylvester and John at the Jesuit College, Liège, Belgium, and taught at Georgetown College, D. C., from the year 1797 to 1819. He died in 1819, and is buried in the College grave-yard. But he was a married man, and his offspring is mentioned on page 16 of this pamphlet.

There seems to have been no other priest in the family until the present time. The Rev. Marshall Boarman is a Jesuit belonging to the province of Missouri, and I belong to the Archdiocese of Baltimore. Father James T. Gardiner, S. J., of the Maryland-New York Province, and Father Edward Dyer, p. S. S., D. D., must be mentioned, for by marriage the Boarmans became related to the Gardiners, just as the Edelins, the Thompsons, the Queens, the Dyers and the Neales—all honorable and respected families of Charles County, Md.